SPOTTED BEAR

A Rocky Mountain Folktale

Hanneke Ippisch

Illustrated by Hedvig Rappe-Flowers

MOUNTAIN PRESS PUBLISHING COMPANY
Missoula, Montana
1998

Designed by Kim Ericsson

Thanks to Christine Paige of Ravenworks Ecology
for reviewing and contributing to "Notes about the Art"

Library of Congress Cataloging-in-Publication Data
Ippisch, Hanneke.
    Spotted bear : a Rocky Mountain folktale / Hanneke Ippisch ; illustrated by
Hedvig Rappe-Flowers.
      p.   cm.
    Summary: A tale that explains how the spotted bear got its spots.
    ISBN 0-87842-387-7 (alk. paper)
    [1. Bears—Folklore. 2. Folklore—Rocky Mountains.] I. Rappe-Flowers,
Hedvig, 1956– ill. II. Title.
    PZ8.1.I698Sp 1998
    [398.2'0978'0452978]—dc21   98-30757
                                                     CIP
                                                     AC

PRINTED IN HONG KONG BY MANTEC PRODUCTION COMPANY

Mountain Press Publishing Company
P.O. Box 2399
Missoula, Montana 59806
406-728-1900

For Les, my man *
—H. I.

For Pat, Erika, and Natalie
—H. R.-F.

* For those of you who might wonder—"my man"
  is an expression of endearment used in the West.

If you walk in the woods at Spotted Bear very quietly and for a long, long time you just might meet a spotted bear.

My man told me about them, and he knows. For he is one of those very quiet sorts who not only listens but also hears, who not only looks but also sees, and who sometimes tells me about things in the woods. When he does, it is as if I receive a rare and secret treasure from a land unknown to most of us.

So, when you walk in the woods at Spotted Bear very quietly and for a long, long time, you just might meet a bear with a bright, white spot right on his chest. And if you listen carefully he might even tell you why he proudly wears that special spot.

8

When there were many bears around, both brown ones and blacks, grizzlies and others, young cubs and old sows, friendly ones and aggressive ones, they lived together rather peacefully in the woods of the north. Of course, at times they argued among themselves, but generally they got along in a friendly manner.

Then came a time when people arrived. They needed to hunt to get meat to eat and furs to keep warm. When the bears felt threatened by hunters, they sometimes attacked them. But mostly the bears lived quietly and took care of their own.

12

It was one of those nights in the forest when the moon was full and when the beargrass bloomed as it only blooms once every fifth year. If you looked very closely, the beargrasses became torches, touched by the moonlight and burning brightly, inviting all creatures of the forest to come and celebrate. You see, it was midsummer night, and great things were going to happen at Spotted Bear.

14

You must not tell anyone, but the midsummer night meeting is held right where the Spotted Bear Land borders Quintonkon, a favorite hideout of spotted bears since long ago.

16

The animals came from as far away as Wickiup and Marmot Mountain, and from distant Kah Peak. Some even traveled all the way from Moose Lake and Devil's Hump, which took several days over high mountains and through deep valleys.

18

First the small bugs and birds arrived, and the mice, snakes, and squirrels. The porcupines, rabbits, and foxes followed. They came crawling, slithering, hopping, jumping, flying, and then settled down. The larger animals came excitedly: the bobcats, deer, and mountain goats. And, of course, the elk, buffalo, and moose arrived.

uch visiting was going on around the grounds and in the trees, where owls and woodpeckers, hawks and eagles were chattering away.

22

Suddenly, all hushed. It became so quiet, you could hear a pine needle drop to the ground.

nd then, the bears came—all marching in behind each other very proudly, because it was their night.

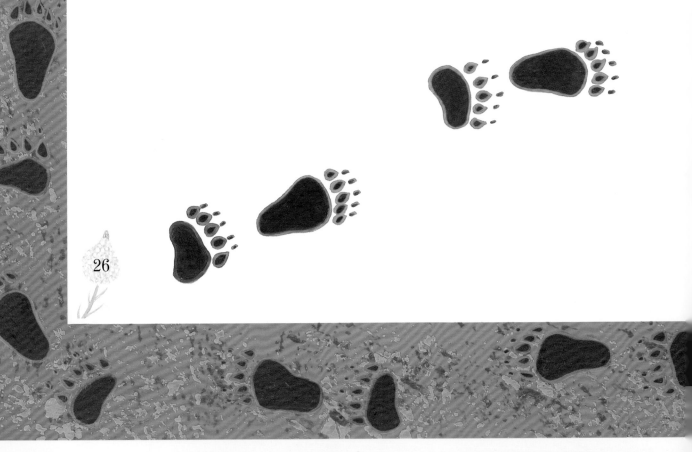

26

**W**hen the beargrass blooms, as it does only every fifth year on midsummer night where Spotted Bear Land borders Quintonkon, there will be some bears chosen as noble bears. They have distinguished themselves through the years by showing extreme courage and restraint toward people.

The time had come to choose the noble bears, and this is what happened:

All the bears slowly marched through the beargrasses, which were glowing as torches lit by the moonlight. Occasionally a beargrass bowed and touched a passing bear on his chest, as if gently stroking him—and when the gently touched bear marched on, a white spot appeared on his chest. He had become a noble bear.

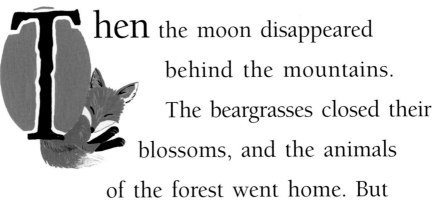

Then the moon disappeared behind the mountains. The beargrasses closed their blossoms, and the animals of the forest went home. But spotted bears—a few—still roam in the woods. I know. My man saw one at Quintonkon Creek many years ago.

**M**aybe you, too, will meet a spotted bear when you are very quiet and walk for a long, long time. And when you do, you will remember that you met one of the very few—a noble bear.

34

About This Folktale

It was early in the morning when Les—my Montana man—and I traveled to Glacier National Park. The sun had barely peeked over the horizon, and Montana was sleepy yet and quiet. We were headed for West Glacier before the stores opened to deliver some of the small wooden creations we make at our crafts workshop, The Schoolhouse and The Teacherage.

Business completed, we were headed toward home when Les suggested that we check out Spotted Bear. He had told me that many years ago he had worked on a dude ranch at Spotted Bear, guiding guests on horseback into the Bob Marshall Wilderness. He also kept busy repairing things around the ranch. I had never visited this place.

The ranger at Hungry Horse told us that the road to Spotted Bear, which is closed during the winter because of heavy snow, had just opened that day. So, we started driving—and driving—for 47 miles on the dirt road that led to Spotted Bear. The woods were full of birch trees, the forest floor was abloom with small white twinflowers, and we never saw any people. It was a magical ride in an enchanted forest.

When we finally arrived at the dude ranch at Spotted Bear, no one was there. We looked around, and Les noticed that all the things he had built so many years ago were still in excellent shape. He felt very good.

We drove another mile to the ranger station at the end of the road. It consisted of ancient log buildings shaded by huge and stately pine trees. The ranger had just arrived for the season. I asked him why this place was called Spotted Bear, but his answer did not satisfy me.

We went back to our car, drove until we found a nice spot to camp under some grand firs, and settled down for the night. But I could not sleep. I kept wondering about Spotted Bear, so

I began to write: "Why the bears at Spotted Bear are spotted bears." This book tells the story I wrote down that night.

Some years later, Les and I drove to Alaska. We stopped at every tourist information center to ask about craftspeople in the area with whom we might visit and share ideas.

One day as we were driving through British Columbia on our way home to Montana, we noticed a caboose parked along the road with a sign on the door that read "Tourist Information." We went in and asked if the clerk could direct us to some local craftspeople. She handed us a piece of paper that read "The Schoolhouse and The Teacherage, crafts." Very surprised, as this was the exact name of our business, we decided to find out about the place. As on our trip to Spotted Bear, we drove for many miles on a dirt road. We met several bears on the road and finally found the old schoolhouse and the teacherage.

We knocked on the door and presented the owners, a middle-aged man and woman, with our business card. They were as surprised as we had been. They asked us in, and we became friends. When night came, they invited us to stay for a supper of moose soup. At supper time, an 84-year-old family friend named Larry stopped by to check on his neighbors (he lived "only" 45 miles away), and he joined us for the meal. In conversation, we learned that our hosts and Larry were very much bear lovers, so I read them my Spotted Bear story. As I read the story, Larry started to smile, and the more I read, the more Larry smiled. When I finished reading, I asked Larry why he was smiling. He answered that as a very small child he was raised by an old Indian chief who told him a similar story.

I realized then that many stories are ancient and few are original. Somehow they find their way to us, and we keep the stories alive by passing them on.

Notes about the Art

The pictures in this book show some of the plants and animals that live in the Rocky Mountains. The next few pages identify what you see in the pictures and also tell you a little bit about the plants and animals—where they live, what they eat (or what eats them), what sounds they make, and other interesting things. See if you can find and name all the creatures you see in this book, then look for them where you live—and watch for them the next time you visit Spotted Bear Land.

PAGES 4 AND 5
Red Squirrel
(Tamiasciurus hudsonicus)
Noisy and quick, this bushy-tailed creature has a coat that can be rusty to dark brown. Whenever you walk in the woods, you will likely hear this squirrel's loud, high-pitched scolding, warning all the forest that you're near. It eats green vegetation and stores seeds and mushrooms to eat during winter. Some people call this squirrel the chickaree.

Bearberry
(Arctostaphylos uva-ursi)
Early fur traders called this plant kinnikinnick, after a Native American name for a plant mixture they smoked like tobacco. The leaves and twigs are food for deer and bighorn sheep. Birds, rodents, and bears love to eat the bright red berries, which is why this plant is called bearberry.

Black Bear
(Ursus americanus)
The black bear can have dark brown, red, blond, cinnamon, or black fur, or a combination. The black bear is a great tree climber. It usually eats vegetation such as roots, berries, seeds, and leaves, but occasionally eats mice and squirrels. In winter, the black bear retreats to a cozy den, where it enters a deep sleep. It does not truly hibernate because its body temperature stays near normal. Black bear cubs are born in midwinter and nurse while their mother sleeps secure in their den. On warm days, the bear may come out to sit on its "front porch" in the sun. Black bears live in 36 states in the United States.

PAGES 6 AND 7
Great Horned Owl
(Bubo virginianus)
The large tufts on this owl's head give the bird its name—but these feather "horns" are not ears. The ears are hidden beneath feathers on the side of the owl's head. This owl's call is a series of five to seven deep hoots: *hoo! hoo! hoo-hoo-hoo! hoo-hoo!* Great horned owls eat mice and rabbits. Do you see the owl feather at the base of the pine tree? Owls' flight feathers are covered in soft tiny hairs that silence the sound of air rushing over their wings so an owl can fly without a sound—the better to swoop on mice!

Deer Mouse
(Peromyscus maniculatus)
Only three to four inches long, this mouse shares the coloring of deer: brownish gray on top and white underneath. The deer mouse has large black eyes like shiny beads and very round ears. It nests in burrows either in trees or in the ground. Flower seeds, nuts, and insects are the deer mouse's food.

Ponderosa Pine
(Pinus ponderosa)
These western trees grow up to 200 feet tall and can be as much as 500 years old. They have long needles. The thick reddish bark looks like puzzle pieces and protects the tree from fires. Put your nose up to the bark of a ponderosa pine and smell it—it smells like vanilla or butterscotch.

Calypso Orchid or Fairy Slipper
(Calypso bulbosa)
This beautiful orchid prefers deep shade in the woods and is pollinated by visiting insects. Can you see why someone thought these flowers looked like a little fairy's slippers? In Greek legends, Calypso was a beautiful sea nymph who stayed hidden on an island—a good name for a flower that hides deep in the woods. Please don't pick fairy slippers because they will not grow back again.

Oregon Grape or Holly Grape
(Berberis repens)
Oregon grape grows low to the ground, with bright yellow flowers that develop into dark blue berries. The leaves are prickly like holly leaves. If cooked and sweetened with sugar, the berries taste like grape juice. Bears eat the berries, but deer and elk don't like them.

PAGES 8 AND 9
Gray Jay
(Perisoreus canadensis)
These bold jays are fun to watch—until they snatch some of your picnic food, which is why they are also called camp robbers. Gray jays eat insects, berries, or whatever little tidbits they can find. They live in mountain coniferous forests. Listen for this bird's soft *wheeoo* whistle or low *chuck*.

Ladybug or Ladybird Beetle
(Coccinellidae family)
These red beetles eat aphids, tiny insects that suck the juice from a plant's leaves. Three thousand ladybugs may protect an acre of trees from aphids. Ladybugs hibernate in clusters under fallen branches or rocks. In the high mountains, grizzly bears flip over rocks to find these swarms of ladybugs, and they lap up the beetles like candy.

Shooting Star
(Dodecatheon pulchellum)
Native Americans roasted and ate the roots and leaves of this wildflower. The bright pink flowers with yellow centers look like small shooting stars flashing across a summer meadow. The flower's pollen is released to the breeze by the buzzing of a bee's wings.

Trillium
(Trillium ovatum)
Some people call this white flower wake-robin because it blooms early in the spring when the robins arrive. Ants eat its seeds. *Tri* means "three," which describes the plant's three leaves and three flower petals.

Glacier Lily
(Erythronium grandiflorum)
Every part of this yellow flower is edible. Deer, mountain goats, elk, bighorn sheep, and bears all eat this plant. Bears dig up and eat the plant's bulblike roots. Glacier lilies bloom in early spring and sometimes pop up through the melting snow.

41

Clematis
(Clematis columbiana)
Clematis is a dainty climbing vine that grows in moist and shady woods in the Rocky Mountains. It has light purple flowers that look like lavender hanging lanterns just before they open into four-pointed stars. The plant's fuzzy seed head looks like a many-legged octopus.

Mountain Bluebell
(Mertensia ciliata)
Bear, elk, deer, bighorn sheep, and marmots all graze on this blue wildflower. Pikas love bluebells and will cut and dry the stems and leaves for hay to eat during the winter.

PAGES 10 AND 11
Monarch Butterfly
(Danaus plexippus)
This common butterfly migrates in the fall, and masses of monarchs sometimes cover entire trees when the butterflies stop to rest. When the zebra-striped caterpillars feed on milkweed plants, they store the milkweed's natural poisons in their tissues. This makes the caterpillars and adult butterflies very untasty to birds. The monarch's bright colors warn birds to stay away!

Wild Rose or Prairie Rose
(Rosa woodsii)
The wild rose provides food and cover for grouse, pheasants, and black bears. Birds find rose thickets a safe place to nest. Get close to a wild rose so you can smell its lovely fragrance—but watch out for the thorns.

Huckleberry
(Vaccinium globulare)
This sweet berry is a favorite of many animals, including bears, deer, birds, and humans. Bears fill up on huckleberries to help them fatten up before winter sets in. People love to eat the berries fresh or in jams, jellies, muffins, pies, hotcakes, and ice cream.

PAGES 12 AND 13
Bear Claw Necklace
Some Native American tribes believe that if you wear a part of the bear you will gain the powers or qualities of that animal. The grizzly bear's long, curved claws can grow to 4 inches—how long is that compared to your fingers?

Arrowheads
Native Americans made arrowheads from flint or obsidian rocks. They used them as tips on their spears and arrows, or as knives and scrapers. Obsidian knives can be as sharp as a surgeon's scalpel.

Birch Trees
(Betula papyrifera)
Beavers love to eat birch wood. The wood is hard, and people use it to make snowshoes, clothespins, canoe paddles, toothpicks, and spools. Native Americans used birch bark to make canoes, baskets, cups, and platters. Birch leaves turn golden yellow before falling off in autumn. Look for the smooth whitish birch bark peeling from the trunk in papery sheets, giving this tree the name paper birch.

PAGES 14 AND 15
Raccoon
(Procyon lotor)
The black-masked raccoon has a very good sense of touch, and when foraging in streams it often finds its food by feeling around among the rocks and mud. Raccoons will eat anything they can get their paws on and are especially fond of fruit, frogs, turtles, crayfish, and eggs. They are expert tree climbers and like to sleep high in trees during the day. Keep your trash cans secure and your camp clean because raccoons love to get into people's food and garbage.

Beargrass
(Xerophyllum tenax)
Bears like to eat the young juicy leaves of this plant in spring. Elk and deer eat the flowers and seed pods. Native Americans used the tough grassy leaves to weave baskets, hats, and capes. Beargrass produces a single flowering stalk that grows 2 to 3 feet tall. Each plant blooms only every five to seven years, but when a hillside of beargrass blooms all at once, it fills the air with sweet perfume.

Northern Lights or Aurora Borealis
Northern lights are a wondrous show of color in the night sky. They are most visible in the far north but can sometimes be seen on dark, clear nights in the Rocky Mountains. They are caused when small electrically charged particles, called electrons and protons, shoot out from the Sun and enter Earth's magnetic field, setting the sky aglow. Northern lights can be green, yellow, red, blue, or violet. They can look like rays or streaks, or like glowing curtains that shimmer and dance. Sometimes they look like the glow of a big city to the north.

PAGES 16 AND 17
American Crow
(Corvus brachyrhynchos)
This is a large, completely black bird with a sturdy bill and strong feet. It makes a nest in a bowl of sticks in a tree. Its voice sounds like *caw* or *kahr*. You will usually see crows in a gang, flying and finding food together. Ravens, the crow's larger cousins, are usually seen alone or in pairs.

Rose Hips
Rose hips are the small, red fruit left after the rose's blossoms have fallen. They are rich in vitamin C and are used in teas and vitamins. Many birds and animals eat the bright hips for their fleshy outer fruit. These rose hips are from the wild rose (*Rosa woodsii*).

Red Fox
(Vulpes vulpes)
The red fox is a clever hunter. It will stalk and then leap on its prey with a high pounce. It eats mice, voles, rabbits, and birds that nest on the ground. It has a high-pitched yowl and a sharp bark. The red fox has reddish fur with black ears, black legs, and a white-tipped bushy tail. The male fox is called a dog fox, the female is called a vixen, and the young are called kits. Look for the fox hunting along fencerows and in fields at dusk.

Chokecherry
(Prunus virginiana)
The chokecherry's red or purple berries are hard to swallow raw because they are so tart, but they taste good when sweetened in pies, jams, and syrup. Fall's first frost also sweetens the berries. Birds and bears like to eat chokecherries, but other parts of the plant contain a poison.

Evening Primrose
(Oenothera caespitosa)
The white blossoms of this flower open in the evening and are pollinated by night-flying insects, especially moths. The blossoms turn pink or red and wilt when the sun shines on them.

PAGES 18 AND 19
Western Tanager
(Piranga ludoviciana)
The western tanager makes a nest of braided twigs, roots, moss, and pine needles high in conifer trees. It plucks berries and insects for food. The male has a yellow body and a bright red head—he looks like he stuck his head in a can of red paint! The female has a greenish yellow body with a grayish back. The tanager's song sounds like *pi-tic* or *pit-i-tic*.

Common Nighthawk
(Chordeiles minor)
This bird prefers to fly at dusk, darting through clouds of insects and snatching them with its small bill and big mouth. The nighthawk nests on the bare ground. Its call sounds like *peent* or *pee-ik*. Watch for the bold white bar near the end of the nighthawk's wings, and listen for the whir of its wings when it dives.

PAGES 20 AND 21
Striped Skunk
(Mephitis mephitis)
The chemical weapon under this fearless creature's bushy tail can be smelled from quite a distance, but it uses it only to defend itself. The skunk eats rodents, eggs, grubs, grasshoppers, and beetles. If you or one of your pets are unlucky enough to "get skunked," a bath in tomato juice will take the smell away.

Bullsnake
(Pituophis catenifer)
Bullsnakes are named for the loud hissing sound they make by blowing air from their lungs through a flap in their windpipe. Bullsnakes eat rodents such as mice and voles. Because of their color and hissing sound, they are sometimes confused with rattlesnakes.

Deerfly
(Chrysops species)
The deerfly is a small horsefly that has a very hard bite.

Moose
(Alces alces)
The moose may look ungainly, but it can stalk very quietly through the forests. It feeds on water plants in summer, so look for it in marshy areas. Sometimes you can see a moose "snorkeling" for plants in a lake. The male moose has big, shovel-like antlers.

Elk
(Cervus elaphus)
In autumn, the majestic male elk makes a bugling call to challenge other male elk to battle for dominance. Even with its large antlers, a male elk can gracefully weave its way through the thick forest. Elk browse on leaves and twigs and graze on grasses and herbs.

Bison
(Bison bison)
These large, chocolate brown animals were once an important source of food, clothing, and shelter for the Plains Indians. The bison has a big hump on its shoulder made of muscles that help hold the animal's enormous head. Often it will use its head and curved, pointed horns to dig through the snow to find grass to eat.

Mule Deer
(Odocoileus hemionus)
When running, this deer springs from the ground on all fours, as if hopping. This funny-looking hop lets the deer turn quickly on rocky hillsides when it is being chased by a predator. It has very large ears that look like a mule's ears and a short tail with a black tip.

Mountain Goat
(Oreamnos americanus)
The mountain goat is a great climber that likes to hang out on high, barren, rocky peaks where it eats mountain plants. Sticky traction pads on the bottom of a mountain goat's hoof help it grip rocky ledges.

Bobcat
(Lynx rufus)
The bobcat is not much bigger than a big house cat. Its tail is so short is looks cut off, or "bobbed." Bobcats hunt mainly at night for squirrels, rabbits, mice, and

even deer. Just like house cats, bobcats like to work out their claws on logs and tree trunks to sharpen them and leave a scent mark.

Red Squirrel
(Tamiasciurus hudsonicus)
Here's the familiar red squirrel again, master of the tree tops. In winter, the red squirrel likes to den in an old woodpecker hole, and it comes out to dig up its caches of seeds, cones, and mushrooms. In summer, the red squirrel will make a leaf nest high in the tree tops for sleeping.

Tracks
A moose, a deer, a bear, a badger, a deer mouse, a small bird, a cottontail, a bobcat, and a mountain lion all left their tracks around the edges of these pages. Can you tell which tracks belong to which animal?

Ord Kangaroo Rat
(Dipodymus ordi)
This kangaroo rat lives in prairies, plains, and rangelands of the western United States. It is mainly active at night, searching for the seeds of grasses and other plants. During the day, the kangaroo rat retreats to a burrow underground to escape the heat and daytime predators. The kangaroo rat comes by its name because of its enormous feet and very long tail that help it bound like a kangaroo.

Jackrabbit
(Lepus townsendii)
The jackrabbit can run up to 40 miles an hour and will zigzag wildly to escape predators. It has larger ears than a cottontail rabbit, making it easy to recognize. Jackrabbits don't dig dens but hollow out a resting spot on the ground where they sleep through the day.

Porcupine
(Erethizon dorsatum)
The porcupine looks like a walking pincushion. Its bristles, called quills, are barbed like fishhooks. The porcupine doesn't throw its quills, but with a good swat of its tail it can fill a curious hand or muzzle with painful bristles. Porcupines spend their time in trees or on the ground eating leaves, twigs, and berries, and they love salt.

PAGES 22 AND 23
Pileated Woodpecker
(Dryocopus pileatus)
The largest woodpecker in the Rocky Mountains, the pileated has a red crest, and the male has a red mustache. The pileated woodpecker prefers to nest in the same tree trunk cavity every year. Pileated woodpeckers chisel out rectangular holes in trees and stumps when they search for insects. They make a triangular hole into their nest cavity. Listen for this bird's call, a ringing *wuck-a-wuck-a-wuck-a.*

Bald Eagle
(Haliaeetus leucocephalus)
The bald eagle is the national bird of the United States. It nests in an enormous platform of sticks that it builds in a tall tree near a river or lake. Adults mate for life and may use the same nest year after year. The bald eagle's head and tail become white by the time it is five years old.

Red-tailed Hawk
(Buteo jamaicensis)
The red-tailed hawk is common throughout the Rocky Mountains. Watch for it soaring over open woods, shrub lands, or fields as it hunts for rodents, birds, rabbits, and other small animals. The top side of this hawk's tail flashes red as it flies. Its voice is a screaming *keeer.*

45

Northern Pygmy-Owl
(*Glaucidium gnoma*)
This small owl nests in old woodpecker holes in trees. The pygmy-owl eats small rodents, small birds, lizards, snakes, and large insects, swooping down on its prey from a hidden perch. Its call is a series of single, mellow toots repeated every two seconds. If it turns its back on you, it seems to stare at you with two black "eye-spots" on the back of its head, the better to startle bigger predators.

PAGES 24 AND 25
Mountain Cottontail
(*Sylvilagus nuttallii*)
The mountain cottontail will often nest in a burrow, a grassy hollow under a bush, a hollow log, or a crevice in a rock. It lines its nest with soft hair. Every summer, it can have as many as five litters of five babies each. The cottontail nibbles on grass, leaves, bark, and twigs.

Carpenter Ant
(*Camponotus* species)
These insects gnaw holes in dead wood, in which they build their nests. They are very large ants, and they work together as a society.

Grasshopper
(**Acrididae family and Tettigoniidae family**)
Grasshoppers are good hoppers and good flyers. They feed on leaves, flowers, and almost any green plants. Birds, fish, and small animals eat them. Listen for the *click-click* sound they make as they fly away, and also look for the hidden colors many grasshoppers have on their hind wings.

Pine Cone
This pine cone is from a ponderosa pine. Squirrels love to eat the pine cone seeds. Look for piles of pine cone scales next to tree stumps where squirrels have had their feasts.

PAGES 26 AND 27
Bear Facts
Can you tell a black bear from a grizzly bear? Color and size can be confusing. Both bears come in many colors, and a trick of light can make a dark bear look blond. Adult grizzly bears have a shoulder hump of muscle and very long claws that make them powerful diggers. The grizzly also has a dished face in profile. Black bears do not have a shoulder hump. They have short claws and a straight face profile.

Bear Tracks
As a bear walks and lopes, it places its hind foot just ahead of its front foot's track. When a bear walks very slowly, it may plant its hind foot exactly in its front track, and you won't see the front tracks at all. A bear's big toe on its front foot is the outer toe—just the opposite of people. Bear tracks usually show claw marks. Look for all kinds of animal tracks in mud or fresh snow.

PAGES 28 AND 29
Gray Wolf
(*Canis lupus*)
The wolf hunts in packs and was once common across the United States. Wolves mate for many years, and pack members are usually family relations. The entire pack helps take care of the young. Gray wolves vary in color and can be gray, brown, or black. When wolves howl, it can sound like a group sing-along. They howl to reinforce bonds in the pack, to find each other when separated, and to mark their territory. Sometimes wolves howl to pull the pack together before a hunt, like a howling pep rally.

Pika
(Ochotona princeps)
The small brownish pika lives in talus slopes and rock slides near forests in the mountains and is quite shy. At the first sign of danger, a pika will let out a series of short squeaks to warn other pikas. In the fall, pikas dry leaves and grass to store in "haystacks" among the rocks. The hay is their food for the winter. Unlike its close relative the rabbit, the pika has very round ears and no visible tail.

Morel Mushroom
(Morchella esculenta)
These mushrooms grow in the woods, along streams, and where the ground has been disturbed, such as by a forest fire. Morel mushrooms are delicious and highly prized, but don't pick them unless you're with a mushroom expert because many types of mushrooms are poisonous.

PAGES 30 AND 31
Polyphemus Moth and Cocoon
(Antheraea polyphemus)
This large brown moth has "eye-spots" on its wings that help scare away enemies. This moth's name comes from the ancient Greek myth about a one-eyed giant named Polyphemus. The moth's larvae feed on maple, birch, and other trees and shrubs. They spin their cocoons on the ground or attach them to a twig.

PAGES 32 AND 33
Little Brown Myotis
(Myotis lucifugus)
This little brown bat likes insects and at night may eat its entire weight in bugs. During the day, it roosts singly or in groups in hollow trees, caves, old mine tunnels, or crevices in rocks or buildings. It hibernates in winter.

Grizzly Bear
(Ursus arctos horribilis)
The grizzly bear lives in remote mountain or tundra wildlands and likes lots of room to roam. A sprinkling of silver-tipped hairs on the coat of this bear give the bear a "grizzled" look. Grizzlies will eat almost anything they can find, especially plants, berries, roots, bulbs, ground squirrels, and carrion. They might "snorkel" in streams for fish or graze through a huckleberry patch.

PAGES 34 AND 35
Western Screech-Owl
(Otus kennicottii)
This small, mottled gray or brown owl with yellow eyes spends its daylight hours in a hole in a tree. It hunts mice and voles at night. Its call is a series of short toots that start out slow and pick up speed like a bouncing ball. Males and females also call to one another with short and long trills, singing in duet.

Ursa Major
Ursa major is a formation of stars, or constellation, that is named after the great bear. (In Latin, ursa means "bear" and major means "greater.") The brightest part of the formation looks like a large water dipper and is known as the big dipper. Look for it in the northern sky.

Underwing Moth
(Catocala species)
You can attract these moths in the woods at night by painting tree trunks or stumps with a mix of brown sugar and rotten fruit. The moth's bright underwing colors sharply contrast with their forewings. The forewings look like the bark of trees that the moth hides on during the day.

About the Author

Hanneke Ippisch, born and raised in Holland, has lived in Montana for 27 years. She loves the land, with its forests, rivers, mountains, and lakes. Her Montanan husband, Les, has taught her many things about his homeland, which inspired her to write *Spotted Bear.* She is also the author of *Sky,* an autobiography of her involvement in the Resistance during World War II. The Ippisches live in a renovated rural schoolhouse near Missoula, where they build and sell fine wooden toys and ornaments and run an award-winning bed-and-breakfast.

About the Illustrator

Hedvig Rappe-Flowers has lived in Montana for 25 years and says the natural world inspires her art. Her acrylic paintings are on view in Montana galleries and graced the poster for the first national conference on watchable wildlife. She holds degrees in fine art and art education. She is the main designer for the Ippisches' schoolhouse market and volunteers as an elementary school art teacher. Ms. Rappe-Flowers lives in Missoula with her husband, Pat, and daughters, Erika and Natalie.